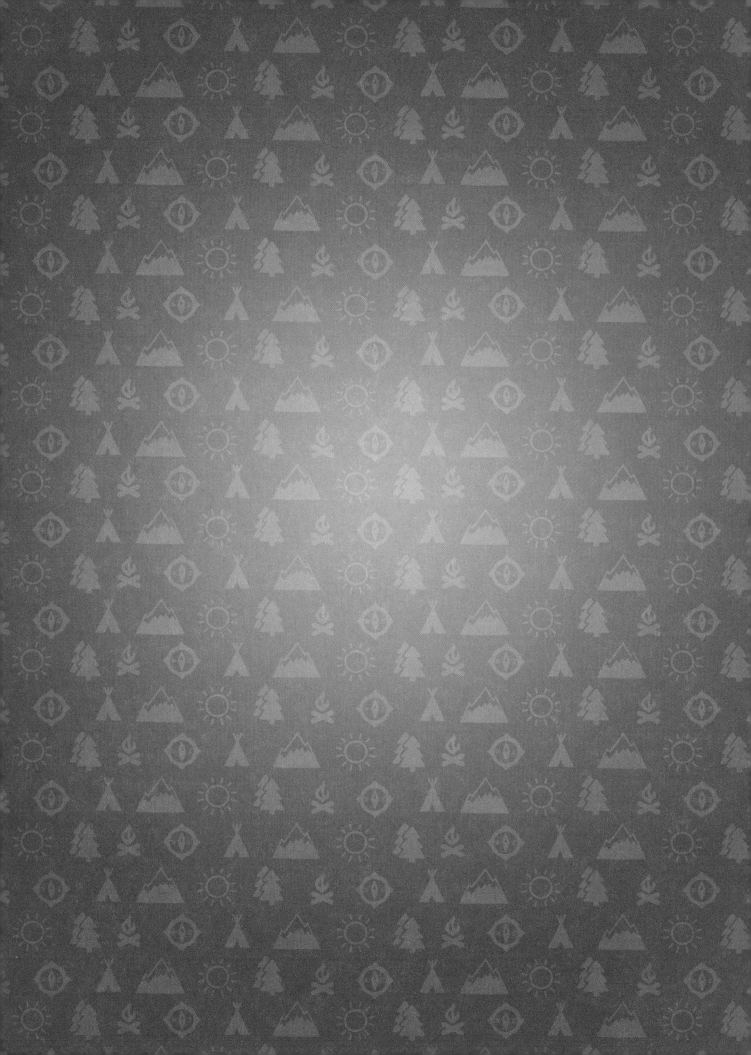

Holy Cannoli Levi!.
Hope this true story
makes you smile
With Best Wishes
Elliot Sloyer

The Safety Pin

by Elliot Sloyer
illustrated by Vic Guiza

Stamford, Connecticut

Library of Congress Control Number: 2014931295
ISBN: 978-1-60131-182-5

Visit us on the web: www.summercampstories.com

The text of this book is set in DIN Condensed
The title of this book is set in Komika Display Wide
Printed in the United States of America
First Edition

Castlebridge® books

115 Bluebill Drive
Savannah, GA 31419 United States

This book was published with the assistance of the helpful folks at DragonPencil.com

To my co-counselor Diane, with love and gratitude on our 25th Anniversary

E.S.

Michell, Sandra and Katherine, enjoy this great and fun adventure

V.G.

David and Elliot were great camp friends. They lived far away from each other during the school year, but every summer they were bunkmates at Camp Massad.

As the weather got warmer and flowers started to bloom, David and Elliot looked forward to reuniting at the camp bus stop. They always sat together on the bus that took them to camp in Tannersville, Pennsylvania.

When David and Elliot arrived at camp, they made sure to get beds next to each other in their bunk.

And when they played sports, they always wanted to be on the same team.

One Sunday, David and Elliot walked together to morning prayers. David brought a safety pin with him from the bunk.

Everybody at camp had safety pins to keep their dirty socks together in the laundry. The safety pins kept the socks in pairs, so that none of them got lost. When clothes came back from the laundry, the socks were clean and still pinned together. The safety pins were sparkling clean too.

During morning prayers, David took the safety pin out of his pocket and started to play with it. First, he opened and closed the safety pin. Then, he started to rub the safety pin against his cheeks. A few minutes later, David put the safety pin in his mouth and began sucking on it as if it were candy.

Elliot knew that putting a safety pin in your mouth is very dangerous, but he was so caught up in the singing, that he didn't notice what David was doing.

Elliot turned and saw that David's eyes were tearing up and his face looked a bit pale.

"David, what's wrong?" Elliot asked.

David was so scared that he could barely speak.

"I think I swallowed the safety pin," he whispered.

You think you swallowed the safety pin?" Elliot screamed.

"Well, actually, I'm sure I swallowed the safety pin," David cried.

"Holy moly!" Elliot said. "We'd better go tell a grown-up right away."

Elliot and David hurried to the back of the social hall to tell their counselor, Solomon, what had happened.

"Is everything okay guys?" the counselor asked.

"David just swallowed a safety pin!" Elliot said.

"He what?" asked the counselor.

"David swallowed a safety pin!" Elliot replied.

"You can't swallow a safety pin. A safety pin isn't food!" the counselor said.

"I know that, . . . but he did!" Elliot shouted.

"Holy cannoli!" said the counselor. "We need to go to the infirmary right away."

7 DAYS WITHOUT PRAYER MAKES ONE WEAK

David, Elliot, and the counselor quickly walked to the infirmary. As they got closer they saw Rebecca, the camp mother, standing on the porch.

"How are you boys feeling on this beautiful day?" she asked.

"My friend David just swallowed a safety pin!"

"He what?" asked the camp mother.

"David swallowed a safety pin!" Elliot replied.

TALENT IS GOD GIVEN – BE HUMBLE
FAME IS MAN GIVEN – BE GRATEFUL
CONCEIT IS SELF GIVEN – BE CAREFUL
J. Wooden

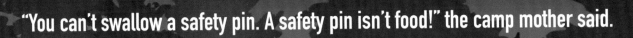

"You can't swallow a safety pin. A safety pin isn't food!" the camp mother said.

"I know that, . . . but he did!" Elliot shouted.

"Holy ravioli!" said the camp mother. "We need to go see the camp doctor right away."

David, Elliot, and the camp mother marched into the infirmary and found their way to the doctor's office.

"How y'all doin'?" Doctor Romanowitz asked with a southern accent, even though he was from Brooklyn.

"My friend David just swallowed a safety pin!"

"He what?" asked the doctor.

"David swallowed a safety pin," Elliot replied.

"You can't swallow a safety pin. A safety pin isn't food!" the doctor said.

"I know that, . . . but he did!" Elliot shouted.

"Holy minestrone!" the doctor said. "We need to get David to the hospital pronto. I'll have Rafi, the camp driver, take us there."

Rafi sped to the hospital as fast as the law allowed.

As everybody piled out of the car, a nurse greeted them.

"Welcome to Allentown Hospital. What seems to be the problem?" asked the nurse.

"My friend David just swallowed a safety pin!"

"He what?" asked the nurse.

"David swallowed a safety pin!" Elliot replied.

"You can't swallow a safety pin. A safety pin isn't food!" the nurse said.

IN TRIBUTE TO
MR. SHUCHATOWITZ

LET YOUR SPIRITS NOT FAIL
COME JOYOUSLY
SHOULDER TO SHOULDER
TO THE PEOPLE'S AID
C.N. Bialik

As the elevator descended toward the basement, David asked, "What's a radiologist?"

"A radiologist is a special kind of doctor who takes pictures of your insides in order to know what's wrong and help you get better," Doctor Romanowitz explained.

When the elevator doors opened, everybody raced to the doctor's office.

"What can I do for you young gentlemen?" the radiologist asked.

"My friend David just swallowed a safety pin!"

"He what?" asked the radiologist.

"David swallowed a safety pin," Elliot replied.

"You can't swallow a safety pin. A safety pin isn't food!" the radiologist said.

"I know that, . . . but he did!" Elliot shouted.

"Holy rigatoni!" said the radiologist. "We need to take some x-rays so we know what's going on."

After studying the x-rays for a few minutes, the radiologist said, "David, I was afraid that you were going to need an operation today and would have to stay in the hospital for a long time. Luckily, the safety pin is closed and it's inside your stomach, so it should come out in a few days. However, if the safety pin doesn't come out in five days, you will need to come back to the hospital to have more tests."

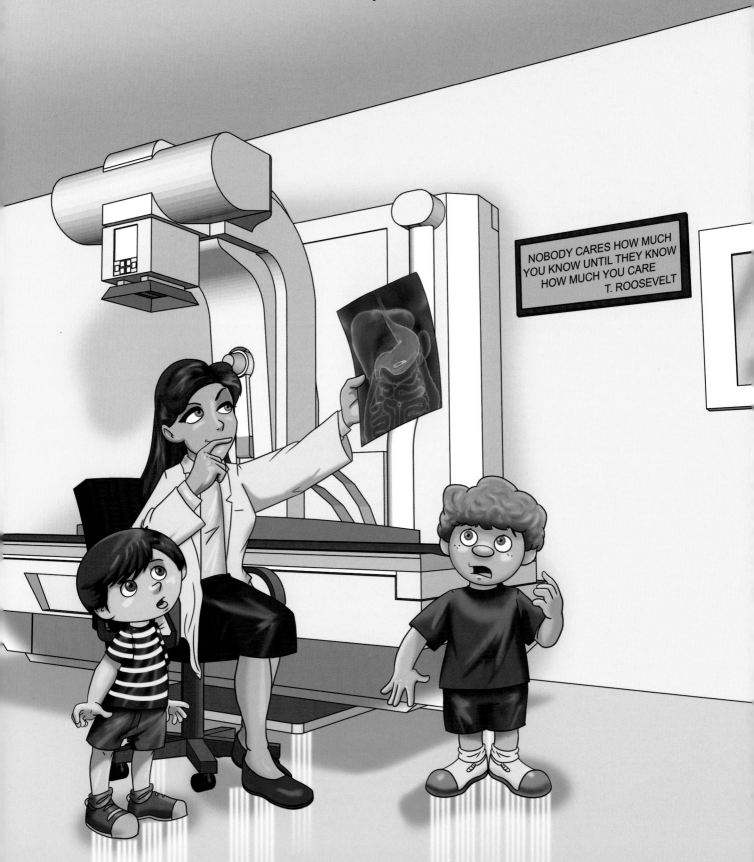

"But how will I know if the safety pin comes out?" David asked.

"Well, David," the radiologist explained, "after you go to the bathroom you will need to look inside the toilet bowl to see if the safety pin came out."

"Yuckity Yuck Yuck Yuck!" David and Elliot shouted in unison.

David and Elliot thanked everybody for their help and happily headed back to camp. Although he was not excited about the doctor's advice, David understood that it was important to follow it if he wanted to get better. He felt relieved that he would be okay as long as the safety pin came out.

So every day David carefully followed the doctor's instructions and looked into the toilet bowl, hoping to see the safety pin.

On Monday David stared into the toilet bowl, but he did not see the safety pin.

On Tuesday David felt discouraged when, again, he saw no sign of the safety pin.

On Wednesday David started to worry that he might have to go back to the hospital for more tests.

But on Thursday, when David looked into the toilet bowl, he saw the safety pin floating in the middle of the bowl.

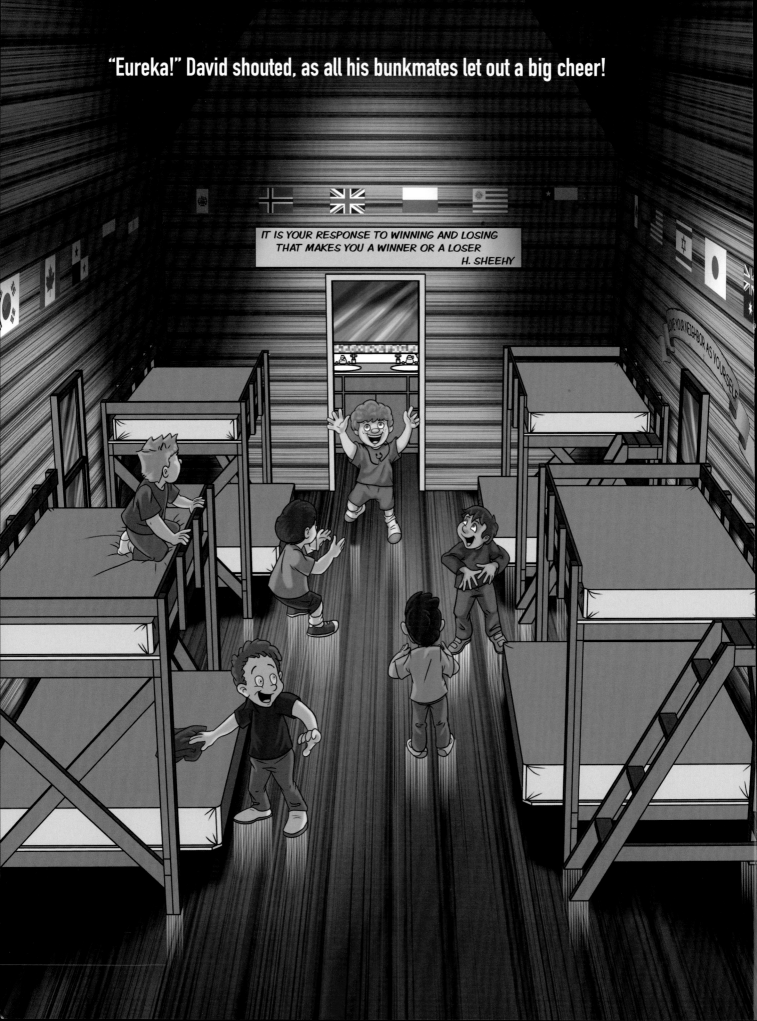

On the last day of camp, David and Elliot boarded the bus to go back home. They were sad that the summer was over, but they were looking forward to seeing their families.

While sitting next to each other on the bus, David told Elliot that every summer he learns a lot of new things at camp. "The most important thing I learned this summer is that it's not safe to put anything in my mouth that isn't food!"

"Holy guacamole!" Elliot laughed. "I thought you already knew that."

GO IN PEACE
RETURN IN PEACE

Thank you!

Amit is Gr8!

COACH LINZER Wins

Is My Hero! Frenkel

EVERYONE ♥ PERLA

For PRESSER President

HANNA & MAZER MAKE YOU

ESSES "THE CEO"

Gets Panoptics It Right!

PITKOFF MVP

Bailey Top Dog

Claude Melody

SOCLOF WINNER

Pomerantz Is Cool!

Jankelovits is #1

Cohen = The Rabbi

the GO TO METZGER Guy!

BENSON is MR. LOYALLEE

LOUZOUN'S NEVER LOSE!

Raymond = Always "MFN"

Brad & Caroline Forever

DOC SCHRAG CARES

RUDY RULES!

DOUECK is Divine!

BODURTHA IS THE BEST

Alvarez is AMAZING

SPILKA IS SUPERMAN!

JUDGE ARNOWITZ

Megan Is Magnificent

Leibowitz The Professor

Howie Judy

ROSENFELD ROCKS

KAHANE is King

QUOTES

1. Love your neighbor as yourself   *~ Leviticus 19*
2. If not now… when?   *~ Ethics of the Fathers 1*
3. Winners never quit and quitters never win
    ~ Vince Lombardi
4. Every strike brings me closer to my next home run
    ~ Babe Ruth
5. Sing to the Lord a new song, sing to the Lord all the earth
    ~ Psalm 96
6. Pray for the peace of Jerusalem, may those who love you be secure   *~ Psalm 122*
7. Seven days without prayer makes one weak
    ~ Church Sign in Louisiana
8. If you will it, it is no dream   *~ Theodor Herzl*
9. Talent is God given – be humble, Fame is man given – be grateful, Conceit is self given – be careful
    ~ John Wooden
10. Let your spirits not fail, come joyously shoulder to shoulder to the people's aid   *~ Chaim Nachman Bialik*
11. Nobody cares how much you know until they know how much you care   *~ Theodore Roosevelt*
12. Things turn out best for the people who make the best of the way things turn out   *~ John Wooden*
13. It is your response to winning and losing that makes you a winner or a loser   *~ Harry Sheehy*